AZZI
IN BETWEEN

WRITTEN AND ILLUSTRATED BY SARAH GARLAND

F

FRANCES LINCOLN
CHILDREN'S BOOKS

There was a country at war,
and that is where this story begins.

It is the story of Azzi.

Every day the war was coming closer to Azzi's house,
yet her life stayed much the same.

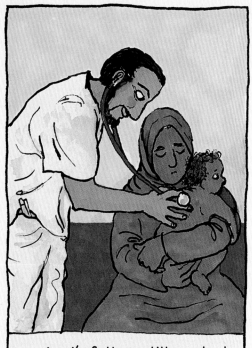

Azzi's father still worked as a doctor.

Her mother made beautiful clothes.

Her grandma wove warm blankets.

In the mornings, Grandma still took Azzi to school.

When she got home, her friends often came around.

Sometimes they looked over the garden wall at the soldiers marching by.

Sometimes the noise of the helicopter gunships was so loud

that the chickens were too frightened to lay their eggs.

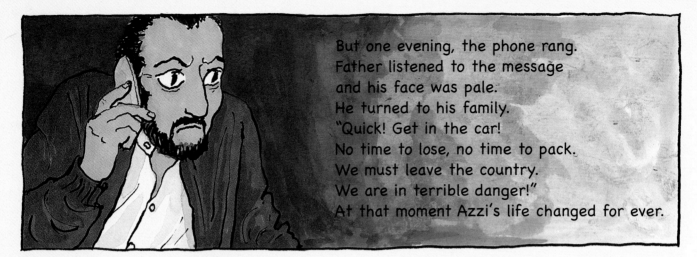

But one evening, the phone rang.
Father listened to the message
and his face was pale.
He turned to his family.
"Quick! Get in the car!
No time to lose, no time to pack.
We must leave the country.
We are in terrible danger!"
At that moment Azzi's life changed for ever.

Father, Mother, Azzi and Grandma ran around the room.
Father picked up a bag of beans. Mother took a blanket, woven by Grandma.
Azzi grabbed her best bear, Bobo. Grandma made Azzi put her coat on.

"I'm staying here, to look after the house," said Grandma,
"It's not so dangerous for me. Don't worry, I'll follow later."
But for Azzi, leaving her Grandma behind was the worst thing of all.

God be with you!

Mother hid Azzi in the car, under Grandma's blanket.

Father drove fast towards the mountains.

Mother sang songs to keep their spirits up.

Once, the car stopped and bright torchlight shone through the windows.
Soldiers shouted, "Show us your papers!" Azzi didn't make a sound.
She knew there were no papers for her and she was scared.
But the soldiers didn't see her.

Father drove on, faster than ever.

How hungry Azzi was, and how thirsty.

She held tight to Bobo until at last she fell asleep.

When she woke, the car had stopped.
Mother opened the door and lifted Azzi out into the cold morning air.
There was the sea, wide and calm.

In the distance a boat was tied to a jetty. People were running towards it.
Father, Mother and Azzi left the car on the beach and they ran too.

On the jetty, the people were shoving and pushing, trying to reach the boat, trying to escape from the dangers of the war.
Father and Mother pushed too, with all their strength.

They struggled down a ladder to the boat and jumped on board.
"That's it! No more!" cried the boatman, as he cast off the mooring rope.
He revved up the engine, the boat turned, and they were out in the open sea.

Up the waves and down the waves, through the days and through the nights, the little boat ploughed steadily across the ocean.

When Azzi licked her dry lips, she tasted the salt sea spray.
When she cuddled Bobo, his fur was stiff with salt seawater.
When she tried to sleep, Grandma's blanket around her was damp and cold.

A new day was beginning. There was only a single star left in the sky.
The land ahead was pink and grey.
For the first time, Azzi saw the shape of the new country.

Everything was different in the new country.
The people looked different.
They gave Azzi food to eat which tasted different.

Can I see your papers, sir?

Men and women talked to Father and Mother in words they couldn't understand.

A man came who spoke their own language. He and Father talked for a long time.

At last a bus arrived to take them to their new home.

But this was very different from their old home. It was small, just one room, with a bathroom on the landing outside.
"Look Azzi," said Mother, "kind people have given us furniture and a cooking pot."
"I'll soon be allowed to work," said Father. "Then I'll make a good home for us."
But Azzi thought, "How can we make a good home without Grandma?"

For many days, Mother and Azzi walked the streets of the big city,
until they were told about a school that had a place for Azzi.

Azzi met her new teacher. He shook her hand and spoke kindly and slowly.
"Hello Azzi. My name is Mr Miller. I look forward to seeing you on Monday."
Mother understood the word 'Monday'. She nodded and smiled.

Mother tucked Azzi up on the sofa on Sunday night.
Azzi was thinking of Grandma, all alone in the old country.

Then she thought about her new school.
How could she make friends when she couldn't speak the new language?
How could she understand her new teacher?

The school was so noisy! Children ran past Azzi. Their clothes were different, their language was different, and nobody stopped to say hello.

A bell rang. Azzi followed the children to Mr Miller's classroom. She frowned. She said to herself, "I will not cry."

Quiet, children!

Mr Miller clapped his hands for silence. He said, "Azzi has joined us today, so please give her a big welcome!" But Azzi couldn't understand his words.

Then, at last, she heard them, words that she could understand,

spoken in a quiet voice, in her own language.

She saw a lady with a kind face, who said, "Hello Azzi. My name is Sabeen. I have come to help you."

Sabeen began to tell Azzi what Mr Miller was saying. She began to teach Azzi some of the new words. Soon Azzi had learned to say 'Hello' and 'Goodbye' and 'My name is Azzi.'

But at lunchtime Azzi felt alone again. She ate the lunch that Mother had made, which was different from the lunches of the other children.

When she had finished, she got her coat from the peg and went out into the playground.

Someone was running towards her. "Hello!" said the girl. "My name is Lucy." Azzi tried to remember Sabeen's lesson. "Goodbye," she said. "My name is Azzi."

"You mean 'Hello'," said Lucy, laughing. "Hello my name Azzi goodbye," said Azzi. Lucy laughed some more, and now Azzi laughed too. "Let's skip," said Lucy.

Azzi watched while Lucy skipped. Lucy counted up to five before she tripped on the rope, so then it was Azzi's turn.

Azzi skipped twenty skips before she tripped on the rope.
That day she had learned another new word, a short word. 'Skip.'

That's a beautiful painting, Azzi!

As the days passed, Sabeen often helped Azzi with her work at school.
One morning Azzi painted her a picture of a helicopter with guns.

I was scared.

Soon Azzi was telling Sabeen the story of the war, and how she had escaped
with Father and Mother, and how leaving Grandma was the worst thing.
"I know how you feel," said Sabeen. "I was only six when we left our country."

Sabeen told Azzi the story of her journey.

"I walked with my family through the forest,

and across rivers,

and over mountains,

until we came to a camp.

We stayed at the camp for many years.

Then I was allowed to leave.

But my family had to stay behind, and that was the worst thing.

One day they will join me," said Sabeen. "And one day I think that you will see your Grandma again."

After that, Sabeen often met and talked to Mother. One day she said, "Azzi is doing really well. Her English is getting better all the time." "I don't want her to forget the language of her own country," said Mother. "No, no!" laughed Sabeen. "She will speak both languages, like I do."

On the way home Mother told Azzi the new words she had learned that day. 'I'd like that one please', and 'How much is that?' and 'Bananas'.

Azzi told Mother the new words she had learned that day. 'Can I have?' and 'What is this?' and 'Grandma'.

When Father came home, he was too tired to tell them the new words he had learned. He lay down while Mother cooked the supper.

"Have you found work yet, Father?" asked Azzi.

"No Azzi," said Father. "I'm still not allowed to work here. If I had a garden, at least I could plant my beans and grow our food. But now my beans are useless. And I have nothing to do." And he closed his eyes.

At school, Azzi began to learn how to count to ten in English. "Soon you will be able to count my toes as well," said Sabeen.

At lunchtimes she often swapped lunches with Lucy.
Lucy said, "I love those chickpeas!"

Then, one warm spring day, Mr Miller talked to the class.
"Tomorrow we will begin our gardening lessons. We will start by sowing our seeds in the school garden. Who will draw some plants that we could grow?"
"ME!" shouted everybody at once.

They drew . . .

a tomato,

a lettuce,

a pumpkin,

and a sunflower.

But Azzi was dreaming. She was dreaming of her garden at home, how the tomatoes turned from green to red, how the lettuce spread its frilly leaves, how the pumpkin climbed up the fence, how the faces of the sunflowers turned to look into the kitchen, where Azzi would sit to eat her favourite meal of spicy beans.

Azzi stood up and walked to the board. She took the pen and drew a bean. "Good girl, Azzi," said Mr Miller. "We can eat that bean, or we can sow it in the ground so it can grow into a tall bean plant, which will give us many new beans." At that very moment, Azzi had her brilliant idea.

Of course! She would get the special beans from Father's bag.

She would plant them herself, in the school garden.

She would give Father a wonderful surprise!

Back in their room, Azzi ran to the bag.

She felt inside. The bag was empty!

And there was a most delicious smell!

"Look, Azzi," said Mother. "I've made your favourite supper. SPICY BEANS!"

Why are tears falling fast from Azzi's eyes?

You must be tired, my love.

Mother doesn't understand it.

It was so hard for Azzi to sit and eat her bowl of spicy beans.
She was thinking about how each one could have grown into a tall plant,
covered with bean pods, and how, by autumn, she could have picked beans
for Mother and Father and the whole school to eat. She could have made
Father happy, as happy as he used to be at home, in the old days.

Azzi couldn't sleep, so she decided to think about the old, happy times. She thought about Mother making her a new dress. She thought about sorting wool with Grandma. But then, as usual, she began to worry. Would they be able to stay in this safe new country? Was Grandma in danger at home?

But Azzi was suddenly wide awake.
There was something under the cushion!

Beans! Fallen from Father's bag.
Lost and forgotten.

Beans that nobody had cooked
and eaten for supper.

Eight perfect beans for Azzi to grow
in the school garden.

She climbed onto the sofa and put
them carefully into her coat pocket.

Now she could cuddle under Grandma's
blanket and sleep happily at last.

Eight beans! Today was the day to plant them.
Azzi pushed eight sticks into the earth in the school garden.
She made a hole for each bean beside each stick.

"Who taught you how to grow beans like that, Azzi?" asked Mr Miller.
"My grandma," said Azzi.
"And now you are teaching us," said Sabeen.

All the way home from school
Azzi thought about her beans
growing in the school garden.

But Mother had a secret too.
She sparkled and smiled in the shop,

Surprise, surprise!

and as they crossed the road,

Are you ready?

right to the door of their room.

She said, "Close your eyes, Azzi."

"Now open your eyes," she said.

Azzi shouted, "GRANDMA!"

And she ran into Grandma's arms. And she cried with happiness.
And Grandma cried with happiness. And so did Mother and Father.

Grandma was very tired, but after supper she told them her story.

"Bad men came to the house with guns. I was very frightened.

I had to leave everything. Our beautiful home, the garden, the chickens.

I sold my golden bracelets to pay for my journey.

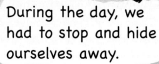

I travelled by night in a big lorry. It was hard and dangerous.

During the day, we had to stop and hide ourselves away.

When I arrived here I was afraid they would send me back.

I felt so happy when they told me I could stay.

We are safe for now and we are together, that's all that matters," said Grandma.

Weeks passed in the crowded room until, one morning, Father's papers arrived. "We can stay!" cried Father. "We are safe! And I can work at last! Follow me!"

They ran out of the door and downstairs, and outside, and round a corner, to a little flat with a yard.

"Now that I can work, we can live here," said Father. "There are two rooms, and a bathroom, and a yard where we can grow our vegetables."
"Space for a sewing machine!" said Mother.
"Space for me to spin!" said Grandma.
"Space for me to skip with Lucy!" said Azzi, and she thought, "My new home will never be the same as my old home, but it is getting better all the time."

All that summer, Azzi learned new things at school.

At home, Grandma told her stories about the old days.

Jamaal arrived, a boy from another country. Azzi and Lucy helped him learn the English language. Jamaal was very good at skipping.

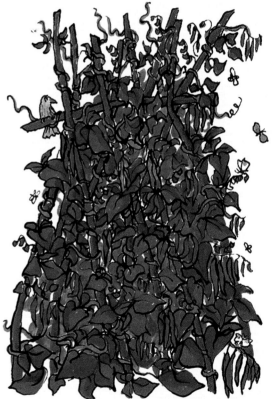

Every day the bean plants grew higher up their sticks in the school garden, and bees visited the flowers, and then green pods hung down, and inside the pods the new beans grew fatter.

Now summer was nearly over. The stems of Azzi's bean plants were brown and dry, and the big beans rattled loosely in their pods.

"In my old country, that means ready to pick," said Azzi.

So all the children, and Mr Miller, and Sabeen, picked the bean pods, and split them open, and filled a bag with Azzi's pink beans.

"Can we keep some to plant in our garden next spring, Azzi?" asked Mr Miller.

"Then, next year, we can grow enough beans to eat for our school dinners."

"I would like that," said Azzi, and she was speaking in her new language.

At last Azzi could take the beans home. Father looked. He looked again.
He ran his fingers through the beans. He said, "But these are just like the beans
I brought from our old country!"
"So they are!" said Azzi. "I found eight of them lost under the sofa cushions,
and I planted them in the garden at school. So now we have a bag full!"
Father kissed Azzi.

He took some beans
to plant in their yard
next spring.

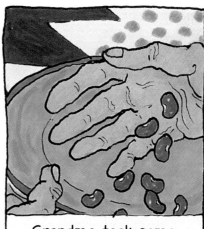

Grandma took some
beans to cook for
supper.

Mother took the
rest to store for
winter meals.

"Are you happy now, Father?" asked Azzi.

"I think you are making me happier, Azzi," he said.

"I'm thinking about a dish of our special spicy beans," said Mother.

"New beans, new life," said Grandma, taking down the cooking pot.

And Bobo smiled, because he always smiled.